QUES
& ANSWERS

about

GROWING

UP

for boys and girls

JOANNA COLE

ILLUSTRATED BY BILL THOMAS

RED
SHED

Originally published in the USA 1988 by HarperCollins*Publishers*
First published in Great Britain 2022 by Red Shed, part of Farshore
An imprint of HarperCollins*Publishers*
1 London Bridge Street, London SE1 9GF
www.farshore.co.uk

HarperCollins*Publishers*
Macken House, 39/40 Mayor Street Upper
Dublin 1, D01 C9W8, Ireland

ISBN 978 0 00 858787 1
Printed and bound in the UK using 100% Renewable Electricity
at CPI Group (UK) Ltd.
001

Consultancy by Professor Michael Reiss

A CIP catalogue record for this title is available from the British Library.

Contents

Introduction

When a family can talk together about sex, there are a lot of benefits. Children learn about an important part of life from people who love them and care what happens to them. Parents (taken throughout this book to mean parents, carers or guardians) make sure their children find out what they need to know as they grow up. Everyone feels good because the 'telephone lines' are open. No one has to be all alone with a question, a worry, or a problem.

But it's not always easy for parents and children to talk. Some parents were raised in homes where sex was rarely, if ever, mentioned. They want to change that for their own children, but it's hard to do. Parents can feel embarrassed or uncertain, and that can make children feel embarrassed, too.

It can help if children understand this about parents. Feeling some shyness about something as personal as sex is common – for adults *and* children. Admitting that you feel awkward can make it easier to talk.

It can be difficult to work out when is the best time to start talking about sex. Schools are a good place to start. They will have information about when sex and relationship lessons will be taught, giving parents a good idea of when it might be helpful to bring up the subject. Of course, if you feel you'd like to discuss sex in your family before it starts to be taught in school, you can – the advice in this book might then be helpful a little earlier.

Some parents say, 'My children don't have any questions about sex'. That is probably not true. Once they have started to learn about sex at school, or hear about it from their friends or on TV, children may well have questions. They just might find it difficult bringing up the subject. Perhaps it has never occurred to them that sex can be talked about openly.

Parents can encourage discussions by letting children know they are available. When sex comes up in conversation, parents sometimes automatically change the subject if children are around. But a parent can use these opportunities to give children information and to open discussions. A parent might say at a moment like this, 'If you have any questions about sex, I'd be glad to answer them'.

It's good to remember that talking about sex is a personal matter. It's healthy to discuss it openly, but everyone has a right to their privacy. Parents are often happy to be asked about growing up, but usually they don't discuss their own sexual experiences with their children. Children want to be accepted when they bring up questions and feelings, but they don't welcome prying. The important thing is for adults and children to share information and values, while respecting each other's privacy.

Some parents think that talking about sex means having one serious session in which the adult tells the child 'everything'. In fact, such a talk will not be all that helpful. Children need to talk about sex and growing up many times as they reach different stages in their growth.

Parents might also not know 'everything'. Often parents feel they are not equipped to teach children about sex. How many adults remember exactly where the fallopian tubes are, which hormone triggers ovulation, or exactly why a boy's voice cracks when it is changing? But this sort of information may not be what is really important when children ask about sex. Biological facts can be looked up if they are needed, but they are often not what children really want. They want a parent to assure them that wet dreams are normal, that puberty comes at different times for different children, that masturbation does not do any harm. They need loving guidance rather than an encyclopedia of sexuality.

The book you are reading now is intended for preteen children. These children may have already started hearing about sex, from TV, the internet and in pop music lyrics. However, this does not always give a healthy or even an accurate view of sexuality as it exists in everyday life. When children learn about sex from adults they know and trust, they learn values along with the facts. They are then less likely to have sex prematurely and more likely to make responsible decisions based on their own best interests as they grow up.

Even though preteens need to be informed, talking with them about sex is not the same as talking with teenagers or adults. Most preadolescent children have not yet experienced intense sexual drives. At their stage of development other issues, such as competence in school and sports and developing social relationships, are far more important than sex. They need to be informed, but they do not want to be overwhelmed by the entirety of adult sexuality. Therefore, the answers in this book are short, geared to the interests and needs of the age.

Some children may be ready to read this book all at once. Others may want to skip around from subject to subject. Or they may read a bit now, put the book away for a year, and rediscover it later, when they have new questions.

Parents will probably want to read this book along with their children, and will also find other books available in the parenting sections at libraries and bookshops. As children move into adolescence, they may want to read some books that deal with the special concerns of teenagers.

In addition to the information children may get in school, from the media, and from their peers, children need loving guidance about sex at home. I hope this book can be a helpful part of the talks between parents and children in your family.

Bodies and Growing Up

As you grow up, your body changes. It is natural for everyone to be curious about what will happen as they grow. You might already have started noticing some changes happening – one change everyone notices is that you keep getting bigger and taller and stronger, as you have been doing since you were a baby. But your body grows in other ways, too. It changes from a child's body to an adult's body. It goes through some changes that make reproduction possible – for the time when you may choose to become a parent. This section is filled with information about what these changes are, when they are likely to happen, and how they are different for boys and girls.

In addition to having questions about their own bodies, young people are usually curious about others. For example, girls might be curious about other boys' or girls' bodies and how they are different from their own. This is natural, too. Let's get started!

What is puberty?

Puberty is the time in your life when your body starts to change from a young person to a fully-developed adult.

What causes puberty to start?

The changes of puberty are started in a small gland at the bottom of your brain called the pituatary gland. This gland releases special hormones (types of chemical that send messages around your body). These hormones travel in your bloodstream to your sex organs (see pages 9–10 and 27), and cause them to release different hormones of their own, called oestrogen, progesterone and testosterone. All of these hormones tell your body to start changing.

Why are our bodies different?

Different people have different sex organs – broadly, penises and vulvas. A boy's sex organs are visible on the outside of his body. Some parts of a girl's sex organs are inside her body, and some are on the outside, between her legs.

Our sex organs make it possible for humans to reproduce (have babies) and to feel sexual pleasure. Different parts of people's sex organs play different roles in the process – the chapters that follow will explain what male and female sex organs look like, and what they do.

Of course, not every person chooses to be a parent,

and not everyone is able to, but all people have sex organs, and most people have sexual thoughts and feelings (though some people never feel sexually attracted to other people – see page 47).

About Girls

What sex organs does a girl have?

Inside her body a girl has two ovaries – oval storage areas for egg cells that may someday grow into babies. She has a uterus – also known as a womb – where a baby grows before it is born. The ovaries are connected to the uterus by the fallopian tubes. And she has a vagina – a passage that leads from the outside of her body to her uterus. Outside her body, between her legs, a girl has an area called the vulva. Within this area is the opening that lets out urine. Just below this, there is a moist opening

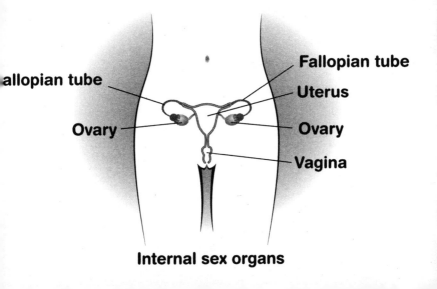

Internal sex organs

– the entrance to the vagina, which leads to the uterus. Just inside the opening of the vagina is the hymen – a thin web of skin that partly blocks the opening. Along the sides of the vulva are folds of skin called labia. There are two sets of folds, the inner labia and the outer labia. Toward the top of the vulva, the labia join together in a V shape. In the V made by the inner labia, there is a small bump called the clitoris. This is very sensitive and can feel nice when it, or the skin around it, is touched. Most of the clitoris is actually inside the body, and this bump is just a small part of it.

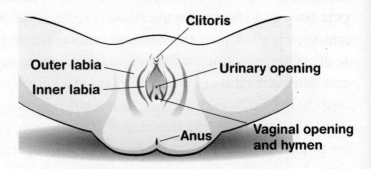

External sex organs

Can a girl see her sex organs?

A girl can't see the organs inside her body, but she can use a small mirror to see her outside sex organs. It's a good idea for girls to get to know what their own sex organs look like. See if you can recognise the different parts – you can use the diagram to help you. Remember that everyone looks a little bit different – for example, some people have larger labia than others.

Does a girl have any other sex organs?

When a girl starts to grow up, the area around her nipples grows into breasts, which can eventually make milk for a baby. Breasts can feel nice if they are touched.

How Girls Grow Up

In the dressing room at the pool, Kayla saw that some girls her age were developing breasts. Others had soft hair growing between their legs or under their arms. Kayla's chest was still flat, and she had no obvious body hair. She worried that she would never grow up.

Kayla felt a lot better when her mother told her that the women in her family usually started developing a little later than most other girls. Starting early doesn't mean your breasts will be larger or you will end up taller.

Between the ages of about eight or nine to about fourteen, a girl's body gradually starts to change. Her breasts grow, body hair begins to develop under her arms and between her legs, she gets a lot taller, her body shape changes, and she gets her first period. Most girls have a mature body by the time they are about sixteen, but changes happen at different times for everyone, so try not to worry if you feel you are starting to change later than everyone else. You can always speak to an adult you trust if you are concerned about anything.

What is usually the first change that happens to girls?

For most girls, the first change of puberty is when their breasts start to develop. This growth can begin from anytime between about age eight and fourteen.

How do breasts grow?

When the breasts first begin to grow, the area right around the nipple gets larger and pushes out in a small mound. As times goes on, the whole breast becomes larger and fuller.

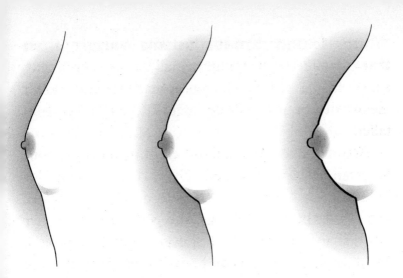

Is breast growth always the first change?

No. Although breast growth can come first, the first change may be the growth of body hair around the vulva or underarm area. It is normal if you begin either way. Everyone's body is a bit different.

Are larger breasts better than smaller breasts?

No. Body shape, breast size and nipple size vary from person to person, and there is no 'better' size. The size of someone's breasts shouldn't affect how comfortable they are, as there are comfortable bras available for all breasts. It also doesn't affect how attractive someone is, because being attractive does not depend on the size of one part of the body.

What if one breast seems larger than the other?

Sometimes a girl worries because one breast seems larger. However, this is normal. The larger breast is simply growing a little faster. Most of the time, breasts are slightly different sizes; no one ends up completely symmetrical.

Do breasts hurt?

Breasts and nipples do not hurt, but they can be sensitive, especially during menstruation (see pages 17–19). Women often try to avoid having their breasts bumped or hit. Some girls find that their nipples are especially tender while they are growing, but many do not feel anything different during this time.

What are breasts for?

If a woman gives birth, special glands in her breasts begin to make milk for the baby. Women can choose to breast-feed their babies or to feed them with a bottle. Breast milk is healthy for the baby, and in the UK it is recommended that babies are breast-fed for their first six months, if it is possible for the mother to do so.

Do women with larger breasts have more milk?

No. A mother's body is usually able to make the right amount of milk for the baby whether her breasts are large or small.

Why do women wear bras?

It is not necessary to wear a bra, but many women prefer to. Some women – especially those with larger breasts – feel more comfortable with a bra. Sports bras give extra support for games, running and other forms of exercise.

When do girls have a growth spurt?

At an average age of eleven, most girls have a growth spurt when they grow extra fast. Girls start their growth spurt about two years before most boys do. So for a while, most girls are taller than most boys their age.

While girls start growing before boys do, they also stop sooner, so boys catch up. Many boys end up being as tall as or taller than most girls.

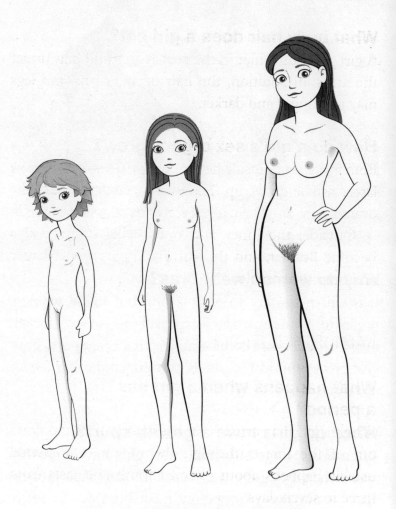

As a girl gets older, she grows taller, and her body changes shape.

How does a girl's body change shape?

As a girl goes through puberty, her breasts get larger and her hips get wider. She gets taller and her body becomes generally more rounded.

What body hair does a girl get?

A girl gets pubic hair in the crotch area and hair under the arms. In addition, the hair on her arms and legs may get longer and darker.

How do a girl's sex organs grow?

Both inside and outside her body, a girl's sex organs grow larger as she grows up. The uterus gets larger, and the ovaries grow and begin to get ready for releasing egg cells.

Outside, the inner and outer labia of the vulva become fleshier, and the vulva and clitoris get larger and more noticeable.

Menstruation

What happens when a girl has a period?

When a girl menstruates (or has a period), blood flows out of the uterus through the vagina. The period usually happens about once a month and lasts from three to seven days.

Why do girls and women have periods?

Menstruation is part of a cycle that the female body goes through about every twenty-eight days to make the body ready for having a baby. The uterus is lined with a thick layer of tissue full of blood. If a woman becomes pregnant, the fertilised egg cell plants itself in this lining and begins to grow into a baby. Then the woman stops having periods and does not menstruate again until after her baby is born.

If a girl or woman does not become pregnant, there is no use for the lining, and it flows out as menstrual blood. This happens from the age of about 12 until about age 51, though specific ages vary.

Do periods always come every twenty-eight days?

Not always. Some girls and women have regular periods every twenty-eight days. Others have regular periods that come at other intervals – say, every twenty-three or thirty days. But many girls' and women's periods are not regular; they start a few days earlier or later every month.

If a girl keeps a record of her periods on a calendar, she can tell what her pattern is. It's a good idea to go and see a doctor if your periods are not following their normal pattern, or are especially heavy.

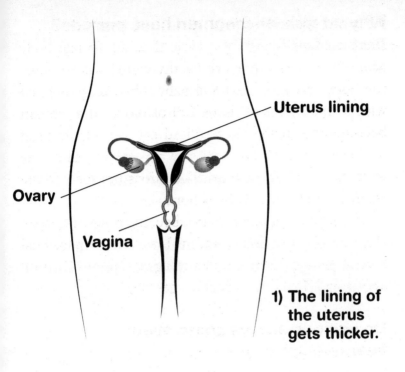

Uterus lining

Ovary

Vagina

1) The lining of
   the uterus
   gets thicker.

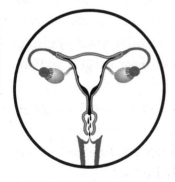

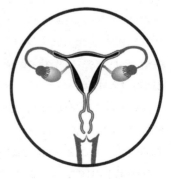

2) If the egg cell is not
   fertilised, the lining
   flows out.

3) Then the lining
   builds up again.

19

At what age do most girls get their first period?

Most girls start menstruating somewhere between the ages of eleven and thirteen, but this is just the average age. Some girls start at nine. Others do not begin until sixteen.

Is having your period like urinating?

Menstruation is different because the fluid comes from the vagina, not the urinary opening. It is also different because menstrual fluid drips out slowly over several days and is not under the girl's control the way urinating is.

Does it hurt to menstruate?

Many girls don't feel anything different during their period, but some girls get cramps in the abdomen. These usually do not last long, and you can try self-care techniques like putting a hot-water bottle on your tummy, or asking a trusted adult to give you some painkillers like paracetamol to help ease the cramps. If the pain becomes too much, a doctor can help.

How does a girl get ready for her first period?

A girl can prepare by getting hold of pads, tampons, period underwear or other methods of absorbing the menstrual flow. Pads and tampons are available to buy at the pharmacy or supermarket, or you can collect them from your school nurse.

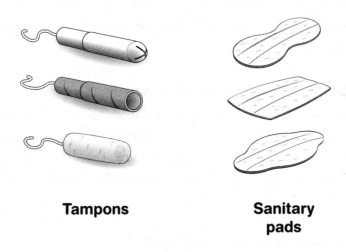

Tampons   **Sanitary pads**

What are sanitary pads?

Sanitary pads, sometimes called sanitary towels or just pads, are made of absorbant material and are designed to catch blood when it flows out of your body. They can be single-use (meaning you throw them away after you use them), or you can get reusable pads that you can wash and use again. Single-use pads have adhesive on one side that you stick to the inside of your underpants. Reusable pads can fasten in different ways, such as poppers. Some pads have wings that wrap around your pants and stick to the underneath. This can help to stop any blood leaking through. You can get pads with different levels of absorbancy – if you have heavier periods, it can help to use pads with a higher absorbancy level.

What are tampons?

Tampons are small plugs of absorbent material that are inserted inside the vagina. When the tampon is inserted properly, it cannot be felt, and it cannot fall out. A short string is usually attached to the tampon and hangs outside. The tampon can be removed by pulling on the string. The advantage of a tampon over a pad is that a tampon absorbs the fluid before it leaves the body, which can make it less likely for blood to leak.

Can girls use tampons or are they only for women?

Most girls can learn to use tampons. There are directions to follow in the box, and you can also ask a parent to help you. There are also slender tampons available that are easier for a young girl to use.

Because there is a disease called toxic shock syndrome (TSS), which has been connected to using tampons, a single tampon shouldn't be kept in for longer than recommended. Women and girls can reduce the risk of TSS by alternating tampons and pads during their period. Some women and girls use tampons during the day, or when they play sports, and wear a pad at night. If you're wearing a tampon at night, put in a fresh one just before you go to bed and change it when you wake up.

How often should I change my pad or tampon?

Tampons and pads should be changed regularly – every 4–6 hours. Make sure to follow pack instructions. Used single-use pads and tampons should be wrapped up in a paper bag (provided in some public bathrooms) or some tissue, then thrown away in the bin. Public bathrooms should have sanitary bins where you can dispose of used tampons and sanitary pads.

Are there alternatives to tampons and pads?

Yes. You can also use period pants, underwear designed to absorb menstrual blood. Using a menstrual cup is also an option – this is a small device shaped like an upside-down bell that fits inside your vagina and catches the blood. Both of these options are more eco-friendly than single-use pads and tampons, as they are reusable.

Is it okay to go swimming, take a bath or shower during a period?

It is fine to go swimming while wearing a tampon. You can also get special period swimwear that act like period pants and absorb the blood. You can take a bath or shower whenever you like. Menstruation is not an illness, and it does not make someone 'impure' or 'unclean'. The best way to handle a period is to do your everyday activities, get some exercise, and live your normal life.

Is it a lot of trouble to have a period?

Caring for yourself during menstruation takes a little thought and effort, but it's generally not that difficult. Menstruation is something that most girls and women learn to manage in the way that's best for them as they grow up.

Does a woman have periods all her life?

No. At around age forty-five to fifty, women stop menstruating and can no longer have babies. This is called menopause. During this process, women might experience symptoms that affect their daily life, including low mood, memory or concentration problems, headaches and difficulty sleeping.

What is perimenopause?

Some women experience symptoms of menopause before their periods stop – this is called perimenopause.

How do girls feel about getting their period?

Every girl has her own feelings about menstruating. If

a girl has not been told about it, she may think she has been injured when she gets her first period. This can be a very scary experience.

In the past, periods were not spoken about openly, but they are a normal part of life for a large part of the population around the world. Periods do not need to be hidden away, and if a girl knows that menstruation is a normal part of being a woman, she can feel proud because it means that she is growing up.

Does a girl become a woman when she starts to menstruate?

A girl still has a lot of growing up to do before she becomes an adult woman who can make grown-up decisions. Once a girl has begun menstruating, it is possible for her to become pregnant and have a baby, but she still has a lot to learn about being a girl before she becomes a woman.

About Boys

In the shower one day, Rajan noticed that his testicles were bigger than before and that the skin of his scrotum was getting wrinkled.

He wondered if this was normal, and since his penis was still small, he wondered why it had not started growing, too. His older brother told him that the testicles usually begin to grow first, about a year before the penis starts to grow or any other bodily changes occur.

Between the ages of about nine and sixteen, a boy's body starts to change into a man's body. His testicles become larger and hang lower, and his penis grows larger. He has a growth spurt and gets much taller, his voice deepens, his shoulders grow broader and his muscles get larger, he gets body hair and often begins to grow a moustache and beard. His body also begins to produce sperm that can combine with an egg cell to start a baby.

What sex organs do boys have?

A boy has a penis and two testicles – oval-shaped organs where sperm cells will someday be made. The testicles are inside a pouch of skin – the scrotum – between the legs.

At the end of the penis there is a small opening where urine and semen (fluid that contains sperm cells) can come out. The penis is very sensitive and can feel nice when it is touched.

Why do some penises look different?

When a baby boy is born, the end of the penis is partly covered by a piece of skin called the foreskin. Sometimes a minor operation is performed on babies to remove the foreskin. This operation is called circumcision.

If a boy is circumcised, his penis will look different from that of a boy who was not circumcised. But their penises are not really different. They work the same and feel the same.

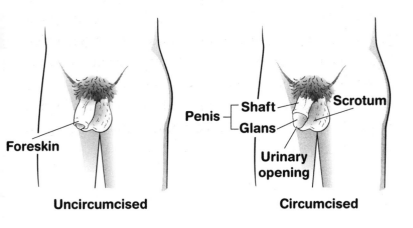

Foreskin

Penis — Shaft — Glans

Scrotum

Urinary opening

Uncircumcised   **Circumcised**

What is an erection?

Usually, a boy's penis is soft. The inside consists of spongy tissue; it does not have any bones. When the spongy inside of the penis becomes filled with blood, the penis gets larger and harder and stands up. This is called an erection.

When do boys have erections?

A boy can have an erection in many different situations. It can happen when he touches his penis, or when he has sexual thoughts. It can happen when his bladder is full, when he is asleep or when he wakes up in the morning. It can happen when he has strong feelings of any kind – when he is nervous or scared or even just excited about playing a game. All men and boys have erections. Even baby boys have them. They are a normal part of being a male.

When does the penis begin to grow?

About a year after the testicles start their growth, the penis becomes longer and thicker. It also changes colour, becoming slightly darker and, in light-skinned boys, redder.

Is there a normal size for a penis?

In grown men, the average size for an erect penis is about 14cm. Some are a bit longer and some are shorter.

If a man's penis is bigger than average when it is soft, will it also be bigger when it is erect?

Not necessarily. You can't tell how big a penis will be when it becomes erect by looking at it when it is soft.

From about age nine to sixteen, a boy's penis and testicles gradually grow larger.

Is the size of a penis important?

No. The size of the penis does not affect life much at all. But some boys worry about it because of stories they hear from other children or read on the internet. For example, they may hear that men with bigger penises have more sperm, that they are more manly or better at having sex. None of these stories are true.

When do most boys start growing taller?

Most boys start having a growth spurt sometime between ages eleven and sixteen, a couple of years after their testicles first start growing. A growth spurt means that they grow extra fast for a few years – usually about 7–10cm a year but sometimes up to 12.5cm a year.

Girls usually have their growth spurt about two years earlier, so for a year or two many girls are taller than most boys their age.

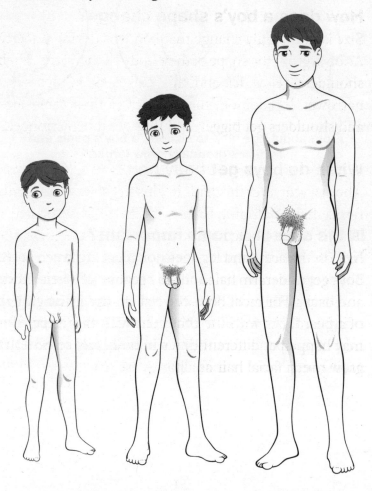

Do boys get stronger as soon as they get taller?

Not always. Sometimes, when boys are in the middle of growing, they get taller so fast that their muscles don't have a chance to keep up. Then a boy may even seem weaker than he was before. This effect is only temporary. Before long, the muscles catch up with the rest of the boy's body.

How does a boy's shape change?

Size isn't the only change that happens during puberty. As boys grow, the shape of their body changes, too. Their shoulders get wider and this makes their hips seem narrower. In addition, the muscles of their arms, legs, and shoulders get bigger, and they get much stronger.

When do boys get body hair?

About a year after the penis begins to grow, boys usually notice hair beginning to grow at the base of the penis. This is called pubic hair. At around the same time, the hair on the arms and legs gets longer and darker. Later, boys get underarm hair and may get hair on their chests and backs. For most boys, the last change is the growth of a beard. (As with the other changes of puberty, this may happen at different times in boys, and some don't grow much facial hair at all.)

How does a boy's voice change?

At the same time as the growth spurt – around two years after the testicles first begin to grow – a boy's voice box grows larger. The vocal cords inside get thicker and longer, and this makes his voice deeper. The cartilage around the larynx can start to show from the outside of the throat – this is called an Adam's apple. While the voice box is growing, some boys find that their voices 'crack' every once in a while. This means that the voice goes from normal to high and squeaky all of a sudden. Voice 'cracking' can feel very embarrassing to some boys, but it is temporary and goes away before too long.

What are sperm?

Sperm are special cells that are produced in the testicles. Every day from the start of puberty, a male's body makes millions of sperm cells, each of which can combine with an egg cell to start a baby.

Can you see sperm?

Sperm are so tiny that they can be seen only through a microscope. Each sperm cell has a head, a midpiece, and a tail. A sperm cell can swim through liquid by lashing its tail.

At what age does a boy's body start to make sperm?

A boy's testicles start producing sperm at the average age of about thirteen, but because every boy develops at his own speed, this can happen a year or two earlier or a year or two later. Some sperm can develop during the first year after the growth of testicles begins.

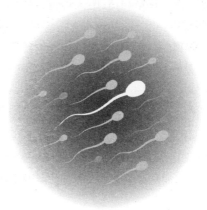

There are millions of microscopic sperm cells in each teaspoonful of semen.

How do sperm leave a boy's body?

Once a boy's body begins making sperm, he will start having ejaculations from time to time. When a boy ejaculates, a thick, white liquid called semen comes out of the opening at the end of his penis. Mixed in the semen are millions of microscopic sperm cells. Even though there are so many sperm, they are so tiny that they fit in a small amount of semen – about one teaspoonful in each ejaculation.

When does a boy ejaculate?

Children sometimes wonder if boys ejaculate when they are urinating. The answer is no. Urine and semen cannot come out of the penis at the same time. A special valve at the base of the bladder closes off the urine during ejaculation.

A boy usually ejaculates when he is masturbating (rubbing his penis for pleasure). He will also ejaculate when he is having a wet dream.

What is a wet dream?

Sometimes, boys ejaculate in their sleep without being aware of it. This happens from time to time for most boys and men. Often a boy will remember having a dream about sex, and that is why night-time ejaculations are called wet dreams. Often, however, there is no memory of a dream.

How do boys feel about wet dreams?

Some boys may feel embarrassed when they wake up and find semen on their pyjamas or sheets. It may help to remember that parents know that night-time ejaculations are normal and happen to all boys as they are growing up.

Does a boy become a man when he begins to have ejaculations?

When a boy begins making sperm and having ejaculations, his body is like a man's in one way: his sperm can fertilise an egg to make a baby. But most boys are about thirteen or fourteen when they begin ejaculating. A thirteen-year-old boy is not ready to take on the responsibilities of an adult. He may be capable of starting a baby, but he needs time to be a child first.

Sex

Is it okay to ask about sex?

Children hear a lot about sex on TV shows, in the news, on the internet, and from other children. Often everyone else seems to know all about everything. You might feel embarrassed to say that you don't know, but inside, you might still like a better explanation.

If you do ask about sex from a good, reliable source – a parent, another relative, a carer, a guardian or a teacher – you might find out that some of the things you heard weren't quite right. You might discover that some of the people who seemed to know everything didn't know so much after all. You might find out that you were worrying about something that you didn't have to worry about.

It is good to have clear, accurate information about sex. It helps you feel comfortable about yourself and your body, and it helps you make better choices about your life as you grow up.

Touching
Feels Good

Before she falls asleep at night, Afia sometimes rubs her clitoris. She likes the feeling it gives her – a wonderful feeling that is not like any other. It makes her feel very excited and then very peaceful and drowsy.

Afia's body and feelings tell her that getting pleasure from touching her clitoris is good. But she has heard some people say it is wrong to do it. She wonders if they are right.

Is it normal to touch your sex organs for pleasure?

Touching your sex organs for pleasure is called masturbation. Many people masturbate sometimes. Some people choose to do it frequently. Others do it occasionally, and some people choose not to do it at all. All of these are valid decisions.

Why do some grown-ups tell children it is wrong to masturbate?

People have different ideas about sex, depending on what they were taught as children. Some people were told years ago that masturbating is wrong, and they still believe it. They might also have their own personal reasons for not masturbating.

If adults tell you it is bad to touch yourself, remember that this may have more to do with *their* feelings than with what is right or wrong for *you*. If you want to masturbate or not is your decision to make.

Does everyone masturbate?

Most people masturbate, but some don't have much interest in it. Others have a religious reason for not masturbating. Some people masturbate at certain times in their lives but not at others. Although many children masturbate, others do not do it at all until they are older. The most important thing is to find what feels best for you.

How do people masturbate?

Different things feel pleasurable for different people – people who decide to masturbate often experiment to work out for themselves what feels nice for them.

Why do people usually masturbate in private?

In our society, sexual behaviour is done in private out of consideration for others. In the UK, it is against the law to masturbate in public places. Privacy also protects the person who is masturbating from being interrupted in his or her intense feelings. *Private* does *not* mean 'secret' or 'sinful'.

What is an orgasm?

Sometimes, a person may have a special feeling of pleasure while they are masturbating or having sex. This feeling is called an orgasm or climax. An orgasm lasts for only a few seconds, but it can be a very powerful feeling. During an orgasm, the brain releases chemicals called endorphins that make people feel happy and relaxed.

During an orgasm, girls and women often feel the muscles in and around their vagina rhythmically contract and release. The clitoris might get larger, and become more moist and lubricated. For boys and men, orgasms usually happen during ejaculation – the release of semen from the penis – although some boys may have orgasms without ejaculating.

For many people, orgasms may not happen until after puberty.

Can it hurt you to masturbate?

It is not harmful to rub your sex organs for pleasure. It does not make you lose any attraction you might have to other people, nor does it make boys run out of semen.

If you enjoy masturbating, there is no health reason not to do it. In fact, when pleasurable, it can be good for wellbeing.

Can a person masturbate too much?

Masturbating does not do any harm to your body, and can be a healthy way to release tension and improve your mood. However, masturbating a lot can be a sign that you are tense or unhappy about something else, and it is possible to become addicted to masturbation. In that case, it can be helpful to try and work out what the cause of those negative feelings might be and get some support, perhaps from a teacher or another adult you trust.

Is it normal to have daydreams about sex?

Yes. Most people have daydreams about sex now and then. They think about going out on dates with people they are attracted to, hugging, kissing or having sex.

Sometimes people daydream about doing something that wouldn't happen in real life. This is nothing to worry about. The important thing to remember is that thinking about something and actually doing it are very different. Your daydreams are your private property. You can have them in private without feeling guilty.

What Is Sexual Attraction?

Every time Olivia sees Alejandro, she can't stop looking at him. She likes his sense of humour, the way his hair grows, the way he smiles. She hopes that he likes her, too, and when she's alone, she daydreams about him.

When a person has these sort of feelings for someone else, it is called sexual attraction, or fancying someone. Fancying someone is often the first romantic feeling children have as they are growing up.

How long do those feelings usually last?

Sometimes people fancy someone for a long time. At other times, their feelings change after a few weeks or months and they become interested in someone new.

Does everyone experience sexual attraction?

Some people fancy lots of different people and spend a lot of time thinking about it. Others only fancy a few people. Some don't experience this sort of attraction. But almost everyone has romantic or sexual feelings at one time or another.

Why don't some adults take children's feelings seriously?

Some adults see a crush as a passing thing, and for this reason they may make light of it or even make jokes about it. Adults who do this, however, are not being very sensitive. Even though children might not be ready to have long-term relationships, their feelings can be powerful and deserve respect.

Why do children laugh about sex or tease others about fancying someone?

Having new sexual feelings can make life more exciting. But it can make things more complicated, too. Children might be curious about sex, but at the same time they may feel a little guilty or embarrassed about it. They might laugh and make jokes about sex to hide their embarrassment. Jokes about sex can be very funny, but if they are just a cover-up for feelings people are ashamed of, they are usually not so funny.

If someone teases you about fancying someone, that person may well have feelings of their own – feelings they want to hide. By making fun of someone else, the teaser hopes people won't notice that they may have a crush on someone, too.

No matter who may tease you, feeling attracted to a special person or people is completely natural. It is nothing to be ashamed of.

Do children ever fancy people of the same sex?

Yes. While it is true that a lot of the time girls are attracted to boys, and boys to girls, children often have strong feelings of attraction for a person of their own sex. This is natural.

Some children may jump to the conclusion that whoever they are attracted to as children will be who they will find attractive as adults. Sometimes this is the case, and their feelings stay the same – sometimes it is not, and who they are attracted to changes over time. Their personal sexual orientation is something for girls and boys to explore at their own pace. Some people are heterosexual, and others are LGBTQ+

(lesbian, gay, bisexual, transgender, queer and other sexualities). To read more about different sexualities, see pages 45–54.

When do girls and boys start going out with others?

Most children feel ready to start going out with others by their mid-teens. Of course, some children of that age may not be interested yet, and, if they are not, there is no reason to rush things.

Going out with someone is a lot of fun, but it takes experience to know what to say and do. It can be helpful for preteen children to get some practice by meeting up in groups.

Is sex appeal the only reason for people to like each other?

Definitely not! Sexual attraction is often part of relationships, but it is not the only part.

Throughout life many people have friends of different genders. Young people also often share the same interests as people they fancy – they might study the same subjects in school, watch the same TV shows, and read many of the same books. They can enjoy spending time together simply because they have a lot in common.

What are good ways for preteens and younger teens to meet socially?

It's fun for preteens and younger teens to have parties with both girls and boys. As children get older, they may meet in small groups at places like the cinema, cafés or at someone's house.

What Does it Mean to be LGBTQ+?

Ava's uncle Harry has always been her favourite relative. He is kind, intelligent and fun to be with. Ava knows that Harry is in a relationship with another man, whom Ava has always called Uncle Leo. Her parents have told her that Harry and Leo are gay.

In school, Ava has heard some children call gay people names. She knows her uncles are good people, and she gets angry because those other children don't understand.

What does LGBTQ+ stand for?

LGBTQ+ stands for lesbian, gay, bisexual, transgender and queer (or questioning). The plus symbol is there to acknowledge other sexual orientations, such as asexuality (see page 47).

What is homosexuality?

Homosexuality is when a person is sexually attracted to others of the same sex. *Homo-* comes from the Greek word for 'same', so homosexuality means having sexual relationships with people of the same sex as yourself.

Homosexual men and women often also call themselves gay, and homosexual women often also call themselves lesbians. What people choose to call themselves is a personal choice and up to them.

What is heterosexuality?

People who are sexually attracted to only members of the opposite sex are called heterosexuals.

Hetero- comes from the Greek word for 'different', or 'other', so heterosexuality means having sexual partnerships with members of the opposite sex.

What is bisexuality?

Bisexual people feel sexually attracted to both men and women. *Bi-* comes from the Latin word for 'two', so bisexuality means being sexually attracted to members of both sexes.

What is asexuality?

Asexual people do not experience sexual attraction towards others (or they might just experience very little). Most asexual people have close emotional or romantic relationships, sex just isn't a big part of these.

What is the difference between sex and gender?

When a baby is born, a doctor or midwife assigns them a biological sex – male or female – by looking at their genitals. There are also other parts of human biology that indicate what a person's sex is, such as their chromosomes (tiny structures in a person's cells that contain instructions about how they develop).

People also have a gender identity that is separate to their biological sex. This is to do with how a person sees and defines themself – for example, if they identify as a woman, man or non-binary (see pages 49–50).

Gender is often seen as binary in society – that people are either male or female. This often means that people are expected to act in certain ways that fit with stereotypes of how people think males or females behave. But how a person presents themselves (for example, how they dress or act) is not connected to their gender. It's up to individuals how they want to define and express themselves. A person's gender can't be assumed by just looking at them – if you want to know what pronouns you should use (she/her, he/him etc), just ask.

What does it mean to be cisgender?

If a person's gender identity matches the biological sex they were assigned at birth, they are cisgender – or cis, for short. For example, if a woman was assigned female at birth, and identifies as a woman in terms of their gender identity, they are cis.

What does it mean to be transgender?

If the sex a person was assigned at birth is not the same as their gender identity, they are transgender – around one per cent of people around the world identify as transgender. Transgender people have a very deep feeling that their biological sex and their gender do not match up. This can cause feelings of distress and uncertainty, called gender dysphoria.

Transgender people may be attracted to the opposite sex, the same sex, or both, just like a cisgender person – whatever a person's sexual orientation, this part of their identity is separate to their gender.

What happens when people transition?

Some transgender people choose to transition, which means they go through a changing process in order to feel closer to their true gender. This process is down to individual choice. Some people choose a medical transition – this might involve taking certain hormones or having surgery. Some people choose a social transition – this might include changing their pronouns (e.g. from she/her to he/him), or using a new name.

Not all trans people choose to transition – they are no less valid as transgender for making this choice. For example, a transgender person might not experience gender dysphoria, so choose not to undergo surgery as part of a medical transition.

Because transitions are a personal choice, asking a transgender person what surgery they have had, or other personal questions about their transition is invasive – let transgender people share any information they want to themselves.

What does it mean to be non-binary?

Gender has often been seen as binary – that people are either men or women. But people are starting to realise that this is not the case, and some people do not identify with either of these genders. Non-binary is a term that covers all genders outside of the traditional male/female binary. This does not mean it's a third gender – it also includes lots of other terms, including gender-fluid, when a person does not identify themselves as having a fixed gender.

Non-binary people do not feel that they are distinctly male or female. They might feel that their identity changes over time, that they have aspects of both genders or neither. Non-binary people don't have to look a certain way – some people assume that non-binary people will look androgynous (neither especially masculine or feminine), but people can be non-binary while also expressing themselves in a traditionally masculine or feminine way. It's all a matter of how they define themselves.

Non-binary people sometimes use the pronouns 'they/them' rather than 'she/her' or 'he/him' to show they don't feel aligned with either gender, but they may also choose to use she/her, he/him or both. The best way to find out what someone prefers to be called is to ask.

Can you tell if someone is LGBTQ+ just by looking?

No. Some people may say that you can tell if a person is LGBTQ+ by the way they look, act and dress. These people may have a stereotyped view that gay men look and act 'feminine', or that gay women dress more like men. But the only way you can find out a person's sexual orientation is if they share it. Everyone expresses themselves differently, whatever sexual orientation they are, and you shouldn't make assumptions.

Has homosexuality always existed?

We know that there were homosexuals in ancient times and that in different times and places, people have had different ideas about homosexuality. In ancient Greece, for example, men sometimes had homosexual relationships in addition to their marriage with women. In some countries in the world today, being homosexual is illegal, making it very difficult for gay people to be themselves.

Why are some people nasty about homosexuality and LGBTQ+ people?

Most people are accepting of LGBTQ+ identities, but there are some people who show hatred and even violence towards people who are LGBTQ+. This is called homophobia. Many also make hurtful, homophobic comments by accident, or assume that gay people will act a certain way because of their sexual orientation, which can be upsetting. This can be for lots of reasons, but may be because most people have grown up with heterosexuality being the default sexuality, and it is only relatively recently that homosexuality has become openly talked about. Some people think there is something wrong or abnormal about being gay, or that acting on homosexual impulses is sinful. If you are an LGBTQ+ person in a difficult situation, talk to an adult you trust.

Can people choose not to be gay?

No one can choose how they feel inside or who they are attracted to. It's just part of who people are, such as hair colour or height. LGBTQ+ people's lives can be very difficult, especially if their family or friends are homophobic, but all sexual orientations deserve to be celebrated, and people should be able to be themselves without fear of being judged by others.

Are heterosexual people ever attracted to someone of the same sex?

Yes. Heterosexual people often have feelings for people of the same sex, they just may not see these feelings to be part of their true sexual orientation. Some people, especially when they are growing up, can have feelings for people of both sexes. It is not unusual for a preteen child to have feelings for someone of the same sex.

Sexual orientation can also change over time – for example, a woman might feel she is heterosexual for a while, then start having feelings for other women. Other people might be very certain of their sexual orientation throughout their whole life.

What if you think you are LGBTQ+?

Your sexual orientation is something for you to explore as you get older, in whatever ways you choose and feel comfortable with. Some preteens may be attracted to people of the same sex and stay with that certain feeling for the rest of their lives. Some might have changing feelings and later be attracted to people of the opposite sex. Whatever your journey, remember that it is yours, and you deserve to feel comfortable in your own skin.

Who you choose to share your sexual orientation with is also your choice. If you are questioning your sexual orientation, it can help to talk to an adult you trust, perhaps a parent, carer or teacher.

Can LGBTQ+ people get married?

In the UK and Ireland, it is legal for gay people to get married. This is not the case everywhere – there are many countries around the world where it is still illegal to marry someone of the same sex, or (in some cases) be gay at all. However, slowly more countries are legalising gay marriage and acceptance of LGBTQ+ identities is growing.

Can a gay couple be parents?

Yes. They can adopt a child, or gay women may choose artificial insemination as a way of becoming pregnant and having a baby. Couples can also make an arrangement with a woman to have a baby for them – this is called surrogacy.

What Is Sexual Intercourse?

In school, Kemi has heard children making jokes about 'doing it'. She knows they are talking about sexual intercourse, and she pretends to know all about it. But at the same time, it's hard for her to imagine having intercourse, and she can't really understand why anyone would want to.

Kemi is not alone in her feelings. Many children don't really understand intercourse, but they feel embarrassed about not knowing, so they pretend to know more than they do.

Why do people have sexual intercourse?

People have intercourse for several reasons. Sexual intercourse is the most common way for a man and woman to start a baby – they might have sex in the hope that the woman will get pregnant. But sex doesn't have to happen just because people want to get pregnant. People of all genders have sex at other times, too, because it feels good or because they find it a good way to express their attraction or love for each other.

What happens when people have sex?

There are lots of different ways that people can have sex, so there is no single straightforward answer to this question. When a man and a woman have sexual intercourse with the goal of making a baby, the man becomes erect, meaning his penis grows harder and

stands up. He then pushes his erect penis into the woman's vagina. Then the man and woman move their hips so the penis slides in and out (without it coming out completely) until the man ejaculates – this means that a fluid called semen comes out of his penis (see p.33).

Sex can also be very different – people don't always have sex because they want to have a baby and it doesn't have to involve a penis entering a vagina. Many people explore what feels best for them with their sexual partner or partners – different things feel good for different people.

Sex can be a very powerful experience between people. Having sexual intercourse is also sometimes called making love, because sex can be a loving experience between two people. It can create strong sexual feelings of pleasure and a sense of closeness for both partners.

Why is it hard for younger children to understand why people have sex?

When young children first hear about intercourse, they often think it is a weird thing to do. This is because they don't know about the *feelings* adults have when they have sex, and they haven't felt the urge to have sex themselves. The actions of having sex don't make much sense if you don't imagine the pleasure that goes along with them. The majority of people start having sexual feelings during their teenage years – but no one has to have sex just because they have the urge to. People should wait until they feel truly ready and comfortable.

Also, because people's sex organs are close to the openings where urine comes out, young children may think that sex is connected in some way with going to the bathroom. As people get older, they understand that sex and going to the toilet are separate functions.

What is consent?

Broadly, consent is when someone freely and openly agrees to something. This is important in all parts of life – for example, you might ask someone if you can take a photograph of them before you take it. Or, you might ask 'would you like a hug?' or 'is it ok if I give you a hug?' before you hug someone.

When it comes to sex, consent is incredibly important. During a sexual encounter, everyone involved has to agree to what is happening, choose to be involved, and be able to freely make that choice. Consent also involves people having the freedom to change their mind, and stop doing what they are doing at any point if they choose.

In the UK, the legal age of consent is sixteen (and seventeen in Ireland), meaning that people under this age can't legally agree to have sexual intercourse. The age of consent is designed to protect children from being abused (see pages 81–84). Choosing to have sex is a big decision – the age of consent is the age at which children are seen to be ready to start making this decision for themselves.

Sex should always be something that everyone involved freely agrees and consents to.

Can children have intercourse?

Children need to grow older before they are ready to have sexual relationships. In the UK, the age of consent is sixteen – in Ireland, it is seventeen. This means that people under this age cannot legally agree to have sexual intercourse.

Do people still have sex when they get old?

Yes. Many people continue to enjoy having sex for as long as they live.

What is a virgin?

Sometimes, the word virgin is used to describe someone who has never had sexual intercourse. However, this term is outdated, and can be used unkindly to suggest that not having had sex is a bad thing. Once people have passed the age of consent, there is no 'right' time to have sex – some people may want to have sex sooner than others. If a person chooses to have sex, they should do so only when they feel ready.

Do some people choose not to have sexual intercourse?

Yes. While most people do have intercourse, some decide not to. Some people are simply happier without sex. Others prefer to wait until they have fallen in love with the right person. Others have religious reasons.

For example, priests and nuns in the Roman Catholic Church take a vow as part of their religion not to have sexual relationships.

Do people have to be married to have sex?

No. Some people believe that unless a couple is married, they should not have sexual intercourse, but many others disagree with this. Many couples who are not married often have sex. Some people believe that you should have sex only with someone you care about deeply and know well.

Before you start having sexual relationships, it is important to know how to prevent pregnancy, which can result from sexual intercourse, and how to protect yourself from certain diseases that can be spread through intercourse. (To read more about avoiding pregnancy, see pages 69–74. For more about diseases that can be spread through sex, see pages 78–80.)

Having a Baby

Rebecca's sister is pregnant, and soon there will be a new baby in the family. At first, Rebecca didn't think about it much, but as time went on, she began to get more excited. She likes to put her hand on her sister's abdomen and feel the baby kick. Now she feels it's somehow 'her' baby and she can't wait for it to be born.

How does a woman become pregnant?

When a woman has sexual intercourse, a sperm cell from the man's body may swim to and join an egg cell, also called an ovum, in the woman's body. When this happens, a new cell is formed that begins to grow into a baby, and the woman starts the early stages of pregnancy.

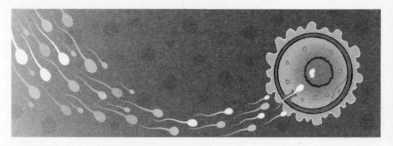

A sperm penetrates an egg cell.

Does a woman get pregnant every time she has sexual intercourse?

No. If an egg cell is not ready in the woman's body when she has intercourse, she will not become pregnant.

However, because it is hard to know exactly when the egg cell will be ready, every time a woman has intercourse, there is a chance that she may get pregnant. For this reason, if a woman and her male partner want to have sexual intercourse but don't want to have a baby, they should use birth control when having sex. (To read more about birth control, see pages 69–72.)

Where in a woman's body does an unborn baby grow?

Young children often think babies grow in the stomach, and even adults sometimes say that an unborn baby is in its mother's 'tummy'. The baby actually develops in the uterus, also known as the womb, which is a special part of the body for babies only.

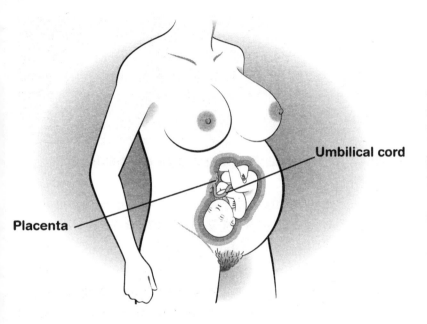

Umbilical cord

Placenta

How does a baby get food and oxygen in the womb?

While the baby is in the womb, the mother's body nourishes the baby. A flat mass of blood vessels called the placenta is attached to the side of the womb. The placenta is the connecting site between the baby's blood supply and the mother's. Through the umbilical cord – a tube that stretches from the baby's navel to the placenta – the baby gets oxygen and nourishment from its mother's blood.

Can a baby move in the uterus?

Yes. After about four months of pregnancy, the mother can often feel little flutters in her abdomen. This is the baby moving. It can move its arms and legs, turn over, even suck its thumb in the womb. Others can sometimes feel the baby moving if they place a hand on the mother's abdomen. Towards the end of the pregnancy, the kicks can be strong enough to startle the mother, but they don't hurt her.

Why are some babies boys and some babies girls?

The baby's sex is determined by the father's sperm. There are two kinds of sperm: some sperm contain the instructions for a baby girl, other sperm have the blueprint for a boy. If a boy-making sperm unites with the egg cell, the baby will be a boy. If it is a girl-making sperm, a girl will be born. Occasionally, babies are born where it is not clear whether they are a girl or a boy – this is called being intersex. Intersex people have a mix of features that are normally associated with being male or female – for example, they might have a penis externally, and also a vagina and uterus internally.

How does a pregnant woman take care of her unborn baby?

A pregnant woman should see a doctor early in her pregnancy – they will organise check-ups throughout the pregnancy to make sure the mother and baby are both healthy. She should eat nourishing food, and avoid drinking alcohol and taking drugs, unless they are prescribed for her by a doctor. Even everyday medicines like aspirin can cross the placenta and affect the baby, so a pregnant woman should not take any medicine without first asking her doctor about it.

How is a baby born?

When a baby is ready to be born, the mother's womb – which has walls made of muscle – begins to squeeze. These squeezes are called contractions or labour pains. Gradually, the womb pushes the baby out and into the vagina, which stretches to let the baby through.

When a baby is born, the uterus contracts and pushes the baby out through the vagina.

What happens if a baby can't come out?

If, for some reason, the birth is difficult, a doctor may perform an operation called a caesarean (or c-section). The mother is given an anaesthetic, and the doctor cuts open the abdomen and uterus. The baby is then lifted out of the opening and the doctor stitches up the incision so it can heal properly.

Does it hurt to have a baby?

Labour contractions – the squeezing of the womb – are often very painful, and labour can last a long time (usually around 8–10 hours for a first baby). But, there are several different ways to ease the pain. People in labour can try techniques like moving their body into different positions, or being in water (either having a bath or giving birth in a special pool). If the pain gets too much, doctors may give them pain relief through methods such as injections, local anaesthetic or gas and air that they can inhale.

What happens to the baby's umbilical cord?

The doctor or midwife puts a clamp on the cord about five centimetres from the baby's belly. Then they cut the cord to leave a stump. Because there are no nerves in the cord, it does not hurt the baby when it is cut. In a week or two, the stump dries up and falls off. Under the stump is the baby's navel.

Why can't some couples have children?

Some couples might not be able to have children because one or both of them are infertile (sometimes also called sterile). Being infertile means that a person cannot have babies. In women, a common cause for infertility is a block in the tubes leading from the ovaries to the uterus. In men, a common cause is low sperm count – too few sperm in the semen.

Same-sex couples and single people are also unable to have children, but might choose other methods such as adoption, surrogacy or artificial insemination, if they would like to have children.

What are some ways for infertile couples to have children?

Many infertile couples adopt babies or older children. Others may go to fertility doctors, who have various methods of improving a couple's chance of having children. A woman may be able to have an operation to unblock her tubes. If the man has a low sperm count, his sperm can be collected and inserted into the woman's womb through a tube instead of through intercourse. Because the sperm are concentrated and now have less distance to swim, there is more chance the woman will become pregnant. This procedure is called artificial insemination.

If the man has no sperm, or if his sperm are unable to penetrate an egg cell, the woman may be artificially impregnated with another man's sperm. If the woman cannot become pregnant, the couple may make an arrangement with a different woman called a surrogate mother – someome who agrees to be artificially impregnated with the man's sperm and have a baby for the couple. The couple can also try IVF treatment (in vitro fertilisation) where the sperm and egg are combined outside of the mother's body, then put back in once the egg is fertilised.

What is a miscarriage?

Sometimes after a woman becomes pregnant, something goes wrong and the developing baby dies. The pregnancy tissue then comes out of the woman's body – the most common symptom is vaginal bleeding.

Miscarriages are sadly reasonably common, and are usually no one's fault. It is often hard to tell exactly why it happens, but it may be because the baby was not developing properly in the womb. Most of the time, a couple will be able to go on to have a baby after a miscarriage, and doctors can offer medical and emotional support.

What is it like to be a parent?

Having children can be a unique and wonderful experience. But parenthood is also a lot of work. Parents must care for their children and give them the things they need. This is a big responsibility, which is why people should think very carefully before they decide to have children.

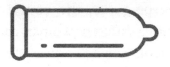

How Do People Prevent Pregnancy?

Marta and Nikhil are a young couple. They are enjoying being together and having sex, but they feel it is too soon for them to have a baby. They want to wait a few years before they start a family, so they are using birth control to prevent pregnancy.

What is birth control?

Birth control is any method a couple uses to prevent an egg and sperm becoming a fertilised embryo. Another word for birth control is contraception. If a man and a woman have sex without using any methods of birth control, it is often called 'unprotected sex'. This is because there is no protection from pregnancy or sexually-transmitted infections.

What are common methods of birth control?

The pill: A woman can take a pill that keeps her ovaries from releasing egg cells. Then it is very unlikely that she will get pregnant. She takes a pill every day. If she stops taking the pills, she will be able to get pregnant again.

The condom: The man puts a rubber sheath – a condom – over his erect penis before intercourse. Condoms also protect against certain diseases. (For more on sexually transmitted diseases, see pages 78–80.)

The diaphragm: The woman inserts a rubber cap – a diaphragm – in her vagina each time she has intercourse. It covers the entrance to the uterus and keeps sperm from entering. To work properly, a diaphragm must be used along with a spermicidal (sperm-killing) jelly or cream.

Other methods: Other types of birth control include contraceptive injections; the implant, which is placed under the skin in the upper arm; a patch that a woman can wear that slowly releases contraceptive hormones; the IUD, a tiny device inserted into a woman's uterus; and the emergency pill (this is sometimes called the morning-after pill, but this is misleading as it can be taken by a girl or woman up to 72 hours after they have had unprotected sex.)

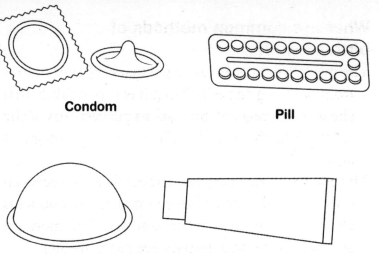

Condom

Pill

Diaphragm with spermicidal jelly

Common methods of birth control are the pill, the condom and the diaphragm (used with spermicidal jelly).

How do people get birth control devices?

Condoms and spermicidal jellies are for sale in pharmacies and anyone can buy them. The pill must be prescribed by a doctor and picked up from a pharmacy. For the IUD, implant and most contraceptive injections, people need to visit a doctor or nurse to make sure they are properly administered or fitted.

People of all ages can get information and birth control devices at GP surgeries or sexual health centres. Children under the age of 16 can access birth control without having to tell their parents or guardians. However, all health professionals have a duty to safeguard children, so they are likely to ask the child about their circumstances and why they need birth control before they provide it.

Which methods of birth control do not work as well?

The rhythm method: In this method, the couple tries to predict when ovulation – the release of the egg cell – will take place in the woman's body. Then they avoid having intercourse at that time. This method doesn't have a very high success rate because it is very hard to be sure when a woman is ovulating.

Jellies and foams: A woman puts a sperm-killing jelly or foam in her vagina before intercourse. These do *not* work well unless a diaphragm is used with them.

Withdrawal: The man pulls his penis out of the woman's vagina before he ejaculates. This is not a reliable method of contraception. It often fails because some semen may escape before ejaculation.

Does everyone use birth control?

No. Some people choose not to use birth control. This may be for religious reasons – some religions teach that it is wrong to try to prevent pregnancy.

What is sterilization?

Sterilization is an operation to prevent pregnancy from occurring. In a woman, a doctor cuts the tubes that lead from the ovaries to the uterus so no egg cells can reach the uterus.

In a man, the doctor cuts the tubes that carry sperm from the testicles to the penis. This operation is called a vasectomy. Semen still comes out of the man's penis when he ejaculates, but there are no sperm in the semen.

People who are sterilized still have sexual intercourse in the same way. The only difference is that a sterilized woman will not get pregnant, and a sterilized man will not make a woman pregnant. For most people, sterilization is permanent; it is an operation that cannot be reversed.

Once a woman is pregnant is there any way for her to avoid having a baby?

Yes. A pregnant woman can have an abortion – a medical procedure to end a pregnancy before the baby can be born. In England, Scotland and Wales, an abortion can be carried out up to 24 weeks of pregnancy, or after 24 weeks in certain circumstances – for example, if continuing the pregnancy would put the mother's life in danger. Two doctors need to give their approval before an abortion can take place. In Northern Ireland, an abortion can happen up to 12 weeks of pregnancy (after 12 weeks in rare circumstances).

Is abortion an alternative to birth control?

Abortion is a procedure that has risks, so people should not think of it as just another method of birth control.

It is an alternative when an unwanted pregnancy has occurred and no other way of avoiding having a baby is possible.

Why does a woman have an abortion?

A woman might decide to have an abortion for a number of reasons. It might be because she has become pregnant without intending to and because having a baby would be a hardship (for example, she might feel she is not in a financially, physically or emotionally stable enough position to raise a child). She might also choose an abortion because the foetus has abnormalities, or because the pregnancy would be dangerous to her own health. Or she might decide she does not want to have a child.

Does everyone agree that abortion is okay?

No. Some people believe abortion is wrong. Some people are against it for religious reasons. Others feel it goes against nature to end a pregnancy. Abortion used to be against the law in the UK, and there are some organizations that are trying to make abortion illegal again.

Other people and groups believe that women have a right to make choices about their lives and their bodies. They do not think that anyone should be able to tell a woman that she must have a baby because she has become pregnant. They feel that this decision is a private one and should be up to the woman.

Getting Pregnant

Greg and Samantha put their arms around each other and kissed. Then they started caressing each other under their clothes. They both thought that they would be able to stop in time, so they did not use any method of birth control. But their feelings were so strong that they did not stop. They had intercourse and Samantha got pregnant. Now they have some potentially life-changing decisions to make.

At what age can a girl get pregnant?
A girl can get pregnant from the age at which she begins to menstruate.

Can a girl get pregnant from kissing or holding hands?
No.

Is it possible to get pregnant the first time you have intercourse?
Yes. Some people might think that you can't get pregnant the first time you have sex, but this is not

true. Some may also think that you can't get pregnant if you have intercourse standing up. This is not true either.

It is also possible for a girl or woman to get pregnant even if her sexual partner pulls out his penis before he ejaculates. Some sperm may come out of the penis before the ejaculation.

Pregnancy may also happen if a male ejaculates while his penis is touching the *outside* opening of the vagina. Some sperm may be able to enter the vagina.

What are the options after getting pregnant?

When a girl or woman gets pregnant, she has three choices. She can choose to have the baby and keep it. She can have the baby and let a family adopt it. Or she can choose to have an abortion. It is likely that her life and the life of the baby's father may change and the decisions involved may be very challenging. If a girl becomes pregnant while she is at school and decides to keep the baby, she will need to consider the impact on her education. If she has an abortion or gives the baby up for adoption, it may have an impact on her and the baby's father's mental health.

Anyone who experiences an unplanned pregnancy, may find it helpful to discuss their options with someone they trust and get support.

Why might someone become accidentally pregnant?

Even if a man and a woman use birth control, there is still a small risk of pregnancy, as no contraception is 100% effective. Unplanned pregnancy can also happen if a couple don't have all the information they need about how to use birth control effectively – GPs and sexual health centres are useful places to get information about how to minimize the risk of pregnancy.

Unwanted pregnancy can also happen after a girl has experienced rape or sexual assault (see page 84).

What is the one sure way to avoid pregnancy?

The surest way to prevent pregnancy is abstinence – not having intercourse.

Diseases You Can Get from Sex

Unfortunately, there are certain diseases that are spread through close contact during sexual activity. They are called STIs, which stands for sexually transmitted infections.

If a person has an STI, there may be itching or sores on the sex organs. Sometimes, however, there are no outward signs or symptoms. But in either case, a person who has an STI can spread it to their sexual partner or partners – STIs are spread through bodily fluids such as saliva, semen and blood.

It is very important for people to go to a doctor or health centre if they think they might have an STI. These diseases can be very serious. It is also a good idea for people who are sexually active to get tested even if they don't have symptoms.

What are the main STIs?

Some of the main STIs are:

AIDS: Caused by a virus; a very serious illness. Symptoms can include a fever, rash and muscle pain. AIDS is not as serious a disease as it once was – it can be successfully controlled using medication.

Chlamydia: Caused by bacteria; may cause infertility;

can be treated with antibiotics. Symptoms can include unusual discharge.

Gonorrhea: Caused by bacteria; may cause infertility; can be treated with antibiotics. It doesn't always have symptoms but people with the disease sometimes notice an unusual discharge when they urinate.

Herpes: Caused by a virus; causes painful sores on the sex organs. It cannot be cured but sores can be controlled by a medication.

Syphilis: Caused by bacteria; can cause serious illness; can be treated with antibiotics. Often causes sores around the penis or vulva.

What is the surest way to protect yourself from STIs?

STIs are transmitted through bodily fluids such as saliva and semen, which can be exchanged between partners during sex. The only completely sure way to prevent STIs is to not have sex, or take part in other practices that might result in bodily fluids being exchanged.

If people do decide to have sex with others, how can they protect themselves?

If people decide they do want to have sexual intercourse, there are measures they can take to protect themselves from STIs. Doctors give the following advice to people who are having sexual intercourse:

* Use a condom when having sex.

• Get tested regularly for STIs. This can be done at a sexual health clinic, or you can order tests to do at home which are delivered through the post.

Are STIs a reason to be afraid of sex?

No, but they are a reason to be *responsible* about sex.

Taking Care of Yourself

When Jada was younger, a babysitter promised to let her watch extra TV if Jada agreed to be sexual with them, touching her body in private places in a way Jada was uncomfortable with.

Jada's parents had told her always to say 'No' if someone asked her to do something that did not seem right, so she refused to do it. Later she told her parents.

When an adult or older child gets involved in a sexual way with a child under the age of 16 (the age of consent in the UK), it is called sexual abuse. It is wrong for people to get sexually involved with children.

What is sexual abuse?

Child sexual abuse is when a child is forced to take part in sexual activities or persuaded to do so. This can happen in person – such as through sexual touching or making a child touch someone else's sex organs. It can also happen through 'non-contact' methods, such as making a child watch sexual videos online.

Who are sexual abusers?

A sexual abuser can be anyone – an adult, a teenager or another child. It may be a man or a woman, a stranger, a family friend or a relative – even a parent or stepparent. There is no way of telling what a sexual abuser may look like.

What is incest?

The word 'incest' means sexual intercourse among members of the same family – brothers and sisters, parents and their children, or other very close relatives. This is illegal in the UK and Ireland.

What is the difference between 'okay touching' and sexual abuse?

Many people use touch as a way to connect with each other and show their love or affection. A friendly, consensual kiss or hug between a child and their parent, relative or friend is not sexual abuse.

Your feelings will often tell you the difference between everyday hugging and kissing and sexual abuse. Everyday touching feels happy, comforting and good. Sexual abuse often feels 'not right'. Remember that you can always say 'no' to being touched or to anything else you don't feel comfortable with.

If you are not sure or feel uncomfortable about

anything that has happened to you, talk to an adult you trust about what has happened, or contact a helpline.

How can children protect themselves from sexual abuse?

Children have a right to say 'No' loud and clear if someone tries to bully them into sexual activity. Abusers can take advantage of a child who is afraid to say no and who won't tell. The best defence is to refuse to keep secrets. Say no and tell a trusted adult – a parent, teacher, doctor or another adult who makes you feel safe. Every child has a right to grow up in charge of their own body.

What should you do if you are sexually abused?

Even when children try to protect themselves, sexual abuse can still happen. If something happens to you, do not let any feelings of embarrassment or fears of being punished stop you from telling someone what happened.

Sometimes children may feel it is their fault if someone forces or tempts them to get involved sexually. But the child is not to blame. The abuser is responsible for what happened. It is very important for children who have been or are being abused to find a grown-up they can talk to and to get help as soon as possible. A child should not have to feel alone with an experience like sexual abuse.

What is online sexual abuse?

Online sexual abuse happens when people trick or pressure children into taking part in sexual activity over the internet, via text messages, emails, online games or using a messaging app.

Some examples might include having sexual conversations, encouraging a child to show sexual parts of their body, sharing sexual pictures of themselves with a child or viewing sexual videos or images. All of these activities are illegal when they involve children. Online sexual abuse is never a child's fault.

What is rape?

If someone makes another person have sexual intercourse when that person does not consent to it, that is a very serious crime called rape. Consent, where both people openly and clearly agree to take part, is a very important starting point for any sexual relationship. If a person does not consent and is made to have sex without wanting to, this is rape. It doesn't matter whether someone knows the person who is forcing them into sexual intercourse or not – whoever is responsible for the rape, it is a very serious crime and should be reported to the police immediately.

The Most Important Thing to Know About Sex

The most important thing to know about sex as you grow up is to respect yourself and others.

Respecting yourself means accepting and celebrating your body. It means making your own choices about what you will and will not do, and not letting others pressure you into something you know is wrong for you.

Respecting others means not teasing or making fun of people about sex. It means making sure you get free, open consent from others in any sexual relationships you might have, and not bullying or tempting another person into having sex against their wishes.

Young people and teens who are able to follow these guidelines are less likely to be hurt or hurt others, and are more likely to have happy, loving relationships as they grow into young adults.

If You Have More Questions

This book tells you a lot about sex and growing up, but it doesn't tell you everything. If you have a question that isn't answered here, you can ask your parents, guardians or carers, a teacher, a doctor or another adult you trust. And you can consult another book. There are many good books about sex for young people at libraries and bookshops.

As you get older, you will have new questions because you'll change and you'll be faced with more decisions. Don't think that you've learned all there is to know about sex just because you've read this book, or because your parents told you about it, or because you have had sex education lessons in school.

Most people keep on learning about sex throughout their whole life. Sex is about people, love, pleasure and intimacy and those are subjects no one ever knows everything about.

Index

Acknowledgments

For their helpful readings of the manuscript, I would like to thank Louise Bates Ames, codirector of the Gesell Institute for Human Development; Bernice Berk, school psychologist at the Bank Street Laboratory School for Children; and Laura Kleinerman, a psychoanalyst in private practice in New York City who has worked extensively with preadolescents. Thanks also to David Reuther for sharing with me his expertise as an editor and as a parent.